Mixing Colours with Red

Vic Parker

Heinemann
LIBRARY

Little Nippers

www.heinemann.co.uk/library
Visit our website to find out more information about **Heinemann Library** books.

To order:
☎ Phone 44 (0) 1865 888066
▤ Send a fax to 44 (0) 1865 314091
▭ Visit the Heinemann bookshop at www.heinemann.co.uk/library to browse our catalogue and order online.

First published in Great Britain by Heinemann Library, Halley Court, Jordan Hill, Oxford OX2 8EJ, part of Harcourt Education.
Heinemann is a registered trademark of Harcourt Education Ltd.

Editorial: Jilly Attwood and Claire Throp
Design: Jo Hinton-Malivoire and Tipani Design (www.tipani.co.uk)
Models made by: Jo Brooker
Picture Research: Rosie Garai and Sally Smith
Production: Séverine Ribierre

Originated by Dot Gradations
Printed and bound in China by South China Printing Company

ISBN 0 431 17341 9 (hardback)
08 07 06 05 04
10 9 8 7 6 5 4 3 2 1

ISBN 0 431 17346 X (paperback)
08 07 06 05 04
10 9 8 7 6 5 4 3 2 1

British Library Cataloguing in Publication Data
Parker, Vic
Mixing Colours with Red
752
A full catalogue record for this book is available from the British Library.

Acknowledgements
The publishers would like to thank Trevor Clifford for permission to reproduce the photographs in this book.

Cover photograph reproduced with permission of Trevor Clifford.

The publishers would like to thank Annie Davy for her assistance in the preparation of this book.

Every effort has been made to contact copyright holders of any material reproduced in this book. Any omissions will be rectified in subsequent printings if notice is given to the publishers.

The paper used to print this book comes from sustainable resources.

Contents

3

The colour red

All of these are red.

Which would you choose to make a red picture?

What is red?

red
grapes

Contrasts

Black and white

red apples

red strawberries

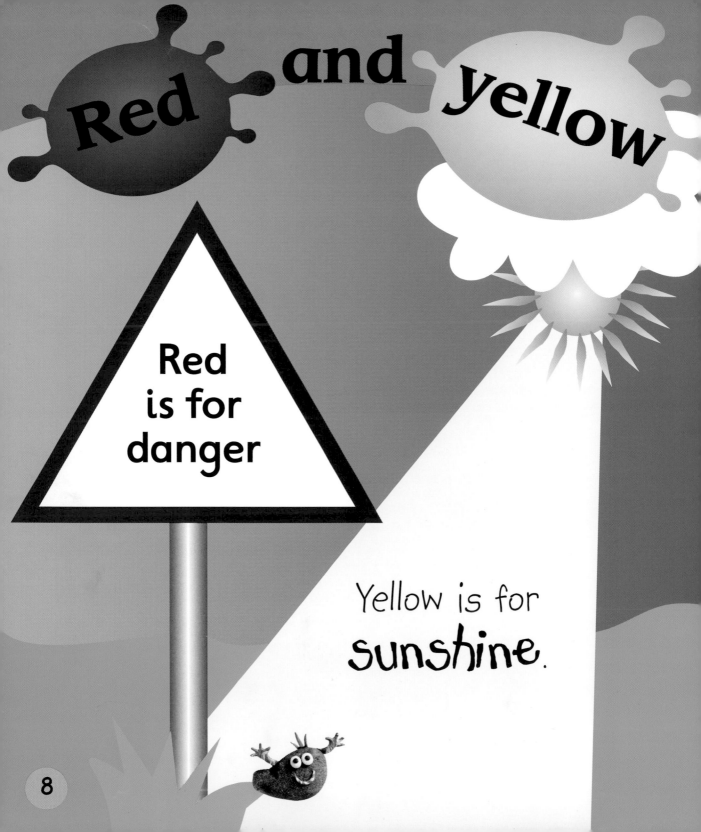

Red and yellow

Red is for danger

Yellow is for sunshine.

8

Mix them together to make
fiery hot orange.

Orange

Orange facepaint is ...

grrrrrr-eat!

11

Red and blue

Dip in ...
dry out.

Dye turns clothes different colours.

13

Purple

Mix red with blue and
what do you get?

purple!

Red white

Yummy white rice.

Scrummy red jam.

16

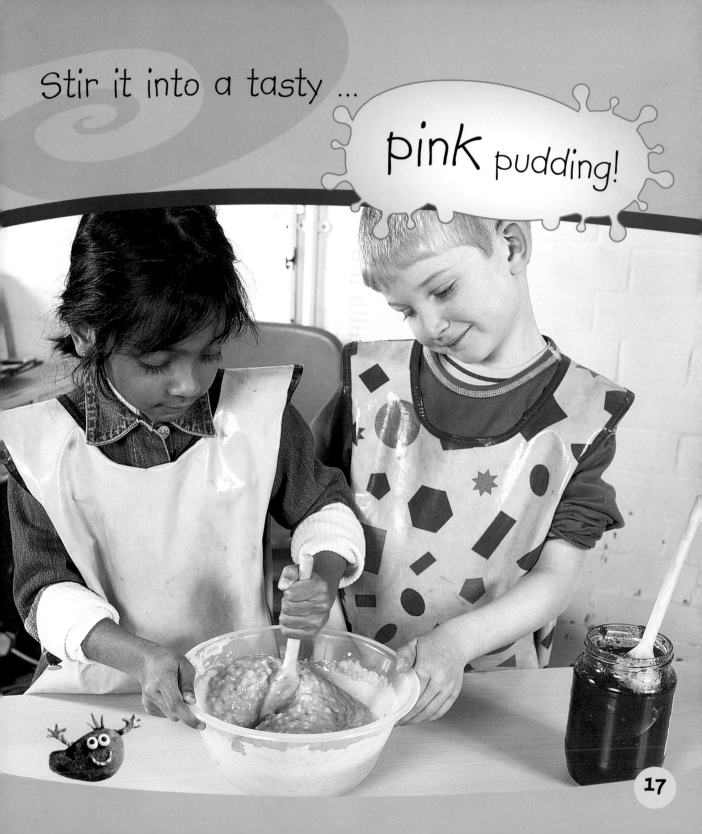

Red and green

Can you guess what they are painting?

ROUNd **red** apples

on a leafy green tree.

19

Brown

Mix together red and green into ...

brown paint for the trunk.

Count the shades

magenta

scarlet

vermilion

color-box

Just right for
red clown mouths!

Index

The end

Notes for adults

The *Mixing Colours* series explores what happens when you blend two colours (occasionally three) together. The books focus on the mixing of pure paint colours, while also leading children to think about other pigments, such as crayons, chalks, pens and dyes. There are four titles in the series, focusing on the primary colours and white. Used together, the books will help enable children to differentiate between colours and begin to understand how they are made. They can also be used to encourage children to talk about what happens when colours are mixed, using appropriate language such as lighter, darker and shade. The following Early Learning Goals are relevant to this series:
Creative development
Early learning goals for exploring media and materials:
• explore what happens when they mix colours
• understand that different media can be combined.

This book encourages young children to think about varying shades of red and which ones they might use to draw or paint red items. It will inspire them to explore what happens when they mix red with other colours, and invite them to experiment with the resulting different colours to make paintings, drawings, collages, constructions, masks and models, etc. The book will help children extend their vocabulary, as they will hear new words such as *crimson*, *scarlet* and *dye*.

Follow-up activities
• See how many red objects your child can find around the house, and compare the shades. You might like to discuss which are orangey-red, pinky-red, or purpley-red, etc.
• Mix red paint with other colours to make orange, pink and purple. Then paint a bright, flowery picture.
• Help your child to draw a big bear's face on some card. Then mix together some red and green paint and paint it brown. (Don't forget some sharp white teeth and fierce eyes!) Cut it out, and attach some elastic, to make it into a scary bear mask.